A Battleaxe and a Metal Arm 20:

Empyrean's End

Samuel Fleming

Cover Art by David Leahey

ISBN-13: 978-1-954679-64-1 (paperback)
ISBN-13: 978-1-954679-62-7 (ebook)

Thank you to my Beta Readers

And, as always, to my First Reader,

Mel.

Contents

"All creatures die, even the
ones that fancy themselves
immortal"
—*Wavering*

Previously...

Helesys sat on the edge of her mother's bed. Despite all the times she had found comfort there in the past, now she found none. She was caught between thousands of years written in stone and an uncertain future. For a brief moment, Helesys spoke with both her mother, Wynbella, and her wand.

But Shawn's arrival in the room helped her see the truth: Helesys wasn't back home in Novissimé—she was trapped inside the dungeon. They were so close to the center that physical dimensions fell apart, and the heroes had to walk through memories to find their way.

But to leave Novissimé, Helesys and Shawn had to fight their way out of the city. For Helesys realized that she would have to repeat the events of that fateful day she left. Guards were no match for them, and eventually Helesys and Shawn leapt from spire walkways, and escaped into the tunnels and sewers beneath the city.

They had to find their way out of the realm. They had to find Taunauk.

The passages beneath Novissimé were ripe with machines and magic that kept the above moving. But there was danger too. Twisted Terrans stalked the passageways—warped by the magic of the Queen. Magic not meant for mortals. The fight was brutal, but Helesys and Shawn hacked and blasted their way through.

Soon, Helesys's memories mixed with Shawn's, and they wandered through the human forge that he toiled away in for so many years. The wisp confessed another of the reasons he left the realm of dreams—fear of twisted creatures, the greatest of these being Nimicus. For all the sadness he found as a mortal, there was salvation in the mundanity of the forge.

When they finally escaped from the tunnels and came to the main gates of Novissimé, they found themselves surrounded by soldiers. This memory was the first time that either had met; the elves had given Shawn the location of Sala Gahenna, but had tried to keep Helesys from leaving. Wynbella finally acquiesced. Helesys saw her mother for the last time, and Wynbella bid Shawn to take of Helesys during their journey.

The forest at the foot of the mountains had transformed into something resembling the Wode. Helesys and Shawn fought more twisted Terrans, this time resembling wolves. They shredded them with blade and wand.

In the twilight of the forest, they found Taunauk and the other Endroggen souls. Spirits had dreamed of their lost loved ones and created a village. Rehkoros led them to Taunauk meditating on the outskirts. They learned that in his memories, Taunauk had ventured to Novissimé looking for Sala Gahenna, but the elves had rebuked him. It was only through Helesys and Shawn that Taunauk had learned the dungeon's location.

Next they came to ruins of the Gatehouse—a fateful spot for Helesys and Taunauk. It was the first they'd learned of the Gatekeeper—now the Queen—and where Taunauk nearly succumbed to a lingering death. There, they found no more answers, only twisted birchmen. Together, the heroes cut them down like wheat.

They reached the edge of the forest and found a field of grass. It was there that they felt overwhelming dread—

For that was where they found Sala Gahenna, and were swallowed by the dungeon.

And it was there they realized that Shawn had gone ahead that fateful day. He had tried to scout ahead and been taken a moment sooner than they. That was why he had been reborn alone so many times.

Despite the overwhelming fear, they prowled forward.

And when they came to memory of Sala Gahenna—the veil hiding the horror—they were nearly trapped again. This time in a loop that would take them back to Novissimé, the beginning of the realm. Instead of going, Helesys tore open the seam, revealing the secret path to the center of the dungeon.

There they found a strange landscape of black glass and shattered sky, and the final castle—dread inducing yet decidedly finite and conquerable.

The heroes traversed impossible realms, faced death and lingering death, and made it to the center of the dungeon. They have come to win their freedom, to kill the Wolf King.

And they finally see an end to their journey.

~ ~ ~

Monument

The heroes walked the plain of perfect black glass to the castle. It loomed in front of them like a dozen daggers sticking in the heart of the world. Skeletons of trees rose up along their path—smooth columns twisting into spider leg thin branches. They were utterly unmoving in the frigid air.

"Are you sure we're in the right spot?" Shawn asked, fastening his cloak tight around him. He slipped twin blades from his pouch before adding, "There might be another ominous castle somewhere farther down."

Helesys stretched her magic senses. "This place is ancient. Even more so than the ashen sea or the river before it…"

Beyond the castle, the realm stretched and blurred. Despite the seemingly infinite realm—unending plain and boiling sky—the castle seemed finite and fixed. It truly was the center of all the worlds in Sala Gahenna—in the dungeon.

It felt as if the whole world was tilted, as if they were standing on the slope and looking down at a bottomless pit. She felt a wake of power flowing to the castle—remnants of what was left after the River of Souls. Flowing to the Wolf King, who sat somewhere in its heart.

"This is it," Helesys said definitively.

The three pressed forward toward the front of the castle. There was an opening in the front wall, some thirty feet square, where a drawbridge or gate might've been. As the heroes passed through, Helesys could feel a raised portion of glass beneath her feet and see the vague outline of seams around the frame.

Moments later, they passed under the gate and the rolling sky above dimmed and died completely. Only the cold followed them inside the castle.

The heroes found themselves in a long, dark hall. Helesys's mind drifted back to those first rebirths stalking the long hall, full of dread. This passage was an echo of those many memories, except even stranger—there were no sconces, no light sources of any kind, yet Helesys could see clearly. Dim light seemed to emanate from the walls, from everywhere and nowhere, all at once. The walls, themselves, were reminiscent of the old bricks, yet they only appeared out of the corner of Helesys's vision—when she looked directly at the wall, the seams faded to smooth purple glass.

The heroes walked in silence; even their footfalls were muted on the glass. Taunauk led, Everfall and axe in hand, while Helesys and Shawn followed with power kindled and blades ready. Both the weaver and rogue kept watch behind them.

Together, they pressed forward into the heart of Sala Gahenna.

With each step, Helesys heart beat faster. Power churned in her metal arm, and she held the Gar of Shéslang tightly. She waited for attack from in front or behind. Waited for any twisted creatures that lurked in the heart of the dungeon.

Despite her apprehension, Helesys felt ready for anything. Even as they walked in ominous silence.

~

The corridor opened up to several large rooms. The light from the walls grew brighter and shimmered like they were holding back murky water. They walked past ghostly furniture—tables and chairs that appeared one moment, and then disappeared out of the corner of Helesys's vision. Taunauk and Helesys walked carefully around the first set of table and chairs, but Shawn curiously touched a chair as they passed. The chair dissolved into purple smoke.

Taunauk glared at the rogue, and Shawn mouthed *sorry*.

They entered a grand dining hall that both towered above their heads and stretched out for hundreds of feet. The grand table was littered with half-finished food and toppled chairs— all of which vanished sporadically at the edges of their vision. For moments, Helesys would smell fruit and seared meat, and then nothing at all. The walls of glass were marred with slightly raised squares—places to mark where tapestries should have hung.

They were halfway through the dining hall when Helesys could bear the uncertainty any longer.

She crept close to Shawn and whispered, "Have you seen anything like this before?"

Shawn shook his head. "It's like walking through someone's half-forgotten dream, but such things are quick to crumble into dust. This has lasted far longer than it should have. Far longer than all the other crumbling realms."

Helesys slowed and her eyes fell across the long glass table and the shadows of food and plates that flickered in and out of existence.

"What is it?" Taunauk whispered to her.

"Just trying to understand our foe. A king in an empty castle."

Shawn replied, "To wield this kind of power, you become removed from the person you once were. It warps and changes a person. Whatever the King was before taking control of this place… I doubt he is a shadow of his former self—less, even.

"But he hasn't forgotten. Not completely," Helesys said to Shawn. "*Half-forgotten dreams*—your words."

Shawn shrugged. "Even a monster may cast a Terran shadow."

"Still," she replied. "It may be something we can appeal to."

Shawn shook his head. "When our opponent might kill us with a thought or a flick of the wrist, it's not wise to hesitate… Never try to bargain with a nightmare."

Taunauk said quietly, "We've seen stranger things in these realms. The king might yet give in to reason or to pity. Failing that, he will bleed."

Taunauk's words fell like an executioner's blade, and he stalked forward once again. Helesys and Shawn followed.

~

They heard the first ghost long before they saw it.

They had reached the end of the massive dining hall when Taunauk spun around, axe at the ready.

Moments later, soft footsteps echoed across the hall and vanished just as quickly. To Helesys, the sound conjured the image of a child running, though she saw nothing.

The heroes waited for minutes with nothing but the sound of their own quiet breathing.

Helesys reached out with magic sense, searching for enemies or ghosts… for anything. "I feel nothing. No traps or enemies. Not even lingering magic within the walls."

When the tension eased, the heroes continued down a short hall and emerged into a grand entryway. Twin staircases rose up the walls, the banisters flickering in and out of existence. An enormous statue stood in the middle, the top of it reaching up past the height of the stairs. Once it might've been a Terran, but now its arms were gone and there was only the slightest hint of face or musculature. The floor looked as though an ornate carpet had once laid there, but was now covered in deep purple glass.

More hallways spread from the large room, but each ended abruptly—as if those wings of the castle had been cut through and then blocked with glass.

The only way forward was up the stairs. Taunauk led them.

All the while, Helesys carried power with her. She'd been waiting. It didn't matter to her that she sensed no traps or enemies—there had to be *something* laying in wait for them. Some minions that the Wolf King would set upon them.

But doubt crept into her mind. Perhaps the Wolf King needed no protection.

They reached the top of the stairs and walked another glass hall filled with half-formed statuettes and blank squares where paintings should've sat. And the farther they walked, the more Helesys felt they were intruding on hallowed ground—like walking over a graveyard.

The hallway led them to a library. Books stretched up ten stories high—all their spines wordless and blurred together into glass. As they walked, Helesys ran metal fingers over a book and it crumbled into dust and smoke.

Twice, she thought she saw a ghost picking through the shelves, but the image was fleeting. Gone in a breath.

Another barren hall led to a worship room. Empty pews and a fleeting ghost kneeling at the altar.

The heroes walked on, paying the memories less and less attention.

~ ~ ~

The Undying Steps

Being on constant guard had made them weary, and Helesys found herself kindling strength to stay alert.

After the worship room and adjoining hall, they came to another grand entryway—

And the end of the castle.

At first, it seemed as if the room was merely large and dark compared to the ambient light from elsewhere in the castle. But as Helesys looked closer, she saw—she felt—that the walls were completely gone. The smooth purple floor disappeared after thirty feet into complete absence. The world beyond the darkness was not merely cloaked in shadow—there was *nothing* beyond it. To Helesys magic sense, it felt like standing next to the edge of a deadly cliff.

There was no ceiling above, only darkness. Only absence.

The only thing in the room was a massive glass staircase. It was so wide that the edges disappeared beyond the darkness, and it rose up into the sky. Helesys craned her neck to follow it, but couldn't see the end. The staircase spiraled upwards, then snaked back and forth into the sky in wide animalistic arcs before coalescing in the center of the sky like a knotted length of yarn.

Before anyone could protest, Taunauk stepped onto the stairs. Helesys and Shawn followed.

They left the ghostly remnants of the castle behind, and though they were climbing above the strange landscape and into the sky, they could see nothing beyond the edges of the staircase. As the staircase spiraled around, even the steps behind them vanished into darkness.

The only thing they saw was the staircase and the infinite steps above. The only thing they knew was upward.

~

They climbed for hours without respite—whether out of eagerness or fear, Helesys couldn't say.

She did not want to give breath to fate.

She only knew the kindling of power to stave off the dull ache in her legs.

"So what's the plan?" Shawn asked suddenly. "We should probably have one of those."

Helesys replied, "We get close enough to use the Machine of Antrikaumora. The king will be powerless."

"The king will be *without magic*," Taunauk replied from the front. "There is a difference between that and being powerless."

Helesys nodded. She knew this to be true. "Magic within us should be unaffected. Your blood magic, Taunauk. Strength from my wand, and your speed, Shawn. But our weapons and projectiles will not work."

Shawn sighed. "So many blades, and you're telling me they won't do me any good?"

Helesys said, "Once the Machine is activated, one blade is as good as another. Our problem will be time. The Machine's power will only last a minute at most."

With that, the conversation died on the stairs. Helesys gave herself to the mundanity.

The heroes climbed so long that they had stowed their weapons. Though they climbed methodically, Taunauk suggested they save their strength. As a result, their pace had slowed somewhat.

They had reached the serpentine parts of the stairs—the way forward curved around viciously upon itself. The perfect spirals were gone completely for as far as Helesys could see. And there was still no end above them.

~

Helesys had nearly lulled herself into a trance, when Taunauk stopped suddenly and slipped axe and shield from his backsling. Beyond the barbarian, Helesys could just see the side of a figure on the edge of the stairs.

Taunauk called to them, "Who goes there?"

Helesys stepped out from behind Taunauk. A young man lay on the stairs. He wore dull silver armor with fading emblems on the chest and shoulders. With a shaking arm, he pulled up the visor of his helmet, revealing pale skin and brilliant purple eyes. His ears were pointed and elven.

The man's breath wavered, and he struggled to reach for the sword sheathed on his hip.

Taunauk lowered his weapons as the man fumbled.

"We mean you no harm," Helesys said, relaxing her gauntlet. "You're injured."

The man startled at her words, then shook his head. *"I'm not injured."* He spoke the old words with faint voice.

Helesys stepped closer. Taunauk and Shawn did the same. She reached out with her magic sense and found that he felt as weak as he appeared. She knelt beside him.

"What's wrong?" she asked.

He eyed each of them in turn like a frightened animal. *"I came to challenge the Wolf King, but… I was afraid."* He breathed deep, as if trying to catch his breath from the climb. *"I am afraid."*

"What's your name?" Taunauk asked.

"Athiden Gorre. I… I must get back to Patrician Sylleth. They must know the truth."

Helesys asked, *"The truth about what?"*

"Sala Gahenna!" he seethed. His eyes grew wide. *"It's not what they think!"*

Helesys rested her hand on his shoulder to reassure him. *"It's alright, Athiden. We know. Can you stand?"*

But Athiden's gaze drifted away, somewhere off into the darkness. *"It's not what they think…"* he muttered.

Behind her, Shawn muttered, "That's no way for someone to go."

Helesys grasped Athiden's arm. *"I'm going to help you stand."*

Shawn said, "Helesys, don't—"

She had already pulled. Athiden's arm extended and then pulled free. Helesys mouth opened in shock as she held the limp arm. It quickly dissolved into smoke and vanished. Athiden still lay on the stairs, muttering to himself in the old words. A moment later, his whole body and armor dissolved into smoke.

Athiden was gone.

Helesys stood, stupefied. She turned to Shawn. "What happened to him?"

Shawn shook his head. "This place hasn't just changed the Wolf King, Helesys. It will change anyone that stays here too long. They'll fade just like the castle." He must've seen her face twisting with regret, because he added, "Athiden was already dead. He just didn't know it yet."

"That's a cold comfort," she replied.

Taunauk said, "We should not linger here."

"I agree," Shawn said. When Helesys didn't move, Shawn asked, "What did he say? Did you know him?

Helesys stared at the spot where Athiden had been. No armor or weapon remained. The glass was perfect—there wasn't so much as a scratch or a speck of dust to mark the elf's passing.

"No," Helesys said, "I didn't know him. But he said he had to get back and talk to the *patrician*. It's an old word for the head of a Great House, back when only males ruled. No one's used the term in a thousand years."

Taunauk said quietly, "The dungeon is old beyond compare. You saw through the eyes of the Idnauthi when it captured their ship. We saw the old gods imprisoned like children."

"I *know*, Taunauk," Helesys said. Even as the words left her lips, she regretted her own tone. "We've seen far more ancient things than an old elf. It's just… To see it is another thing entirely. To feel history slip through my hand… I have no words. I only know that this place has plagued my people for far too long."

She expected Taunauk or Shawn to retort. For Taunauk to tell her that it *changed nothing*, or to remind them *to task*.

In the end, her comrades merely waited silently. They all knew what needed to be done. Sometimes, the most powerful words were the ones not spoken.

~

They continued up the winding glass stairs. There seemed no end above and nothing but darkness below—nothing to mark how far they'd come.

And Athiden was not the only damned soul they passed:

A woman whose skin was gray and rough as stone. She slept on the stairs and didn't stir as they passed. Her hair was a shimmering silver and the tattered braids draped over her chainmail.

A tall, thin figure in a dark cloak lay on their stomach, as if their strength had left as they crawled up the stairs. They looked up as the heroes passed—their pale face twisted in curiosity, eyes weeping green tears.

A strange, gangly creature that reminded Helesys of the Angel beneath Civirrea. Where the other had been shrouded in light, this was laid bare. Its dark skin was dry and cracked, revealing sparks of light beneath. It breath was raspy and chaotic, and it lay unmoving.

Twin men, wearing matching golden armor. One cradling the other's head. The sitting man looked to the heroes, each in turn. *"You can't go back,"* he said in the old words, his voice barely a whisper. *"You can't go back."*

Two other figures lay sprawled on the glass, but dissolved into dust before Helesys could see more than their outline.

"Too afraid to die. Too afraid to live," Shawn said reverently.

Taunauk grunted curiously, but kept walking up the stairs.

Shawn went on, "All the Chosen make this climb. These were the poor bastards that stopped halfway. Too afraid to face the Wolf King, but they couldn't go back. So they just fade away."

The higher they climbed, the fewer damned souls they passed. There were humans and elves, but other strange creatures as well. Winged men, and one centaur-like Terran they'd seen immortalized in stone in the cannibal jungle. None spoke, and most dissolved as the heroes passed, as if they were so old, so weak, that a passing breeze was their undoing.

"Don't stop," Shawn muttered to no one in particular.

Helesys had no intention of stopping. Taunauk didn't so much as pause his steps.

The heroes ascended. Unflinching and unfettered.

~ ~ ~

The Seat of Empyrean

They climbed so long that Helesys stopped looking upward. Her world became endless toil undercut by dull burn in her legs and kindled strength.

She thought only of the climb—only of escape.

They climbed so long that when the stairs ended, it took all three of them by surprise. The heroes walked out onto a platform suspended in darkness. Towering double doors stood in front of them, made of nearly the same featureless glass as the rest of the castle—

Except that the outline of a single wolf's head spanned both doors. The etching was impossibly faint now, worn by the same inexorable time that had whittled the rest of the realm. If there had been any other details in the room, she might've missed the engraving.

The three stood for a long moment, merely staring at the door.

Helesys forced herself to breathe steady and suppressed a chill. She didn't think of how far they'd walked, how much they had struggled, suffered, and overcome. Nor did she worry about the Wolf King or dying at his hand.

There was only the door—only this moment.

She asked, "Are we ready?"

Shawn nodded and pulled his hood back, revealing his wispy hair. "No use in waiting," he said, slipping twin knives from his pouch.

Taunauk merely grunted, his eyes fixed high on the faded wolf engraving. The squeeze of his hand around the leather grip of the axe answer enough.

Helesys stepped forward, testing the door for traps or latent magic—found nothing. She placed her metal hand against it and pushed. The door was heavy, but groaned deep and long as it yielded to her.

Darkness lay beyond.

Before Helesys could kindle her warding light, a voice called from the black.

"Step forward."

Helesys knew the voice, though he spoke the common tongue: *The Wolf King*.

Helesys, Taunauk, and Shawn crept forward into the gloom.

The king appeared some hundred feet away, sitting on a simple stone throne. Long fingers gripped the armrests. Even sitting, he seemed as tall as them—a thin giant of a man. He wore only a deep blue robe and the white wolf mask.

"I have watched your journey with bated breath," the King said. "The Vessel, the Made-thing, and the Wisp. A formidable group. No wonder you think you can succeed where so many others have fallen short."

Helesys reached out with her senses and found no traps or kindled power. No artifacts at his side. No one else stood in the throne room, save for them and the king.

"What's the matter, Helesys Byyra? Did you expect more? I need no trinkets or baubles to kill the likes of you."

Helesys tried to meet the King's eyes, but found only voids behind the mask.

"Are you ready to die?" she asked.

The King held her gaze, then stood. In a single, smooth motion, Helesys felt her heart drop—all three heroes raised their weapons.

The King merely stood. Even from afar, he loomed over them. The throne dissolved, and he walked off into the darkness, leaving the heroes with weapons at the ready.

"Let me show you what happens to those who think themselves *Chosen*."

Darkness fell away, receding over the landscape like an ebbing tide. A cold desert of black glass and starless night stretched out as far as Helesys could see.

The Wolf King stood some half mile away, his white mask a pinprick against the black. Then he stretched out his arms and Helesys felt a pulse of magic though she couldn't hear his words.

"Be ready for anything," she said, as much to herself as to her comrades.

Scattered stars appeared in the sky, and Helesys kindled power as the dots of light began to grow.

The first grew until it was a newborn sun. It blazed with brilliant light—blotting out the darkness. Then the sky began to scream.

A meteor.

Smoke trailed, and the sound grew deafening as the meteor careened into the center of the battlefield. The heroes crouched low as it impacted. Powdered glass exploded into the air, and tremors shook the ground, nearly knocking Helesys over. In seconds, a crater a hundred feet wide had been gouged into the realm.

Helesys looked up in time to see three more meteors growing large in the sky—only now there was no darkness above.

The entire sky was filled with ominous dots of light, thick as sand glistening on a beach. The sky looked like a veil stretched and about to tear.

"Mother of Movernus," Shawn whispered.

In spite of her awe, Helesys steeled herself. They had known the Wolf King would conjure horrors against them; it seemed a fitting display. She couldn't directly counter the spell—not from so far away, nor would her *ice wall* protect them.

She reached for the jade lemur statue in her pocket. Its power was fleeting and there was no promise that it would get them high enough and away from the blasts…

She reached out her magic sense—even as another meteor crashed and blew chunks out of the landscape. She felt the unmistakable touch of magic in the blasts and in the meteors themselves—they were conjured magic!

Instead, Helesys pulled out the Machine of Antrikaumora. Even as she grasped the tiny metal cube, it seemed to answer with power. The red engraving lines pulsed with light. *Antimagic.*

Taunauk and Shawn huddled close as the sky filled with meteors. White sky turned to a rolling sea of fire. They had only moments.

The old words came to Helesys and as she spoke, she swore she heard the faint voice of her wand overlapping her own.

"Non est hic potestas sed meum!"

There is no power here but mine.

The red lines of the Machine flared like vessels burst, and the metal grew ice cold in her mundane hand. Haze surrounded the heroes. The meteor impacts grew faint—the sound muted, the tremors lessened, but not gone completely. Muted by the Machines antimagic powers.

Helesys's metal arm grew heavy and numb, and she had to concentrate on holding onto the Gar of Shéslang.

A sky of rock and fire rained down on them.

All around, meteors crashed into the battlefield, blotting out the Wolf King and the realm. The world became a cloud of muted destruction.

Shattered glass was hurled into the air. Chunks sailed toward the heroes, but when they met the antimagic enclosure, the dark purple rock disintegrated into dust and vanished soon after.

Helesys watched as one meteor fell directly on top of them—wide enough to blot out the sky. She recoiled and winced, even as the meteor crashed into their haven and turned to powder.

Shawn burst into laughter and cheers. Helesys breathed deep. Taunauk stood unflinching; waiting.

They were surrounded by fire and death, and completely unharmed. Only the slightest tremors of impact and whispers of blasts reached them.

The barrage of chaos could have only lasted moments, but to Helesys it felt like eternity. She counted fifteen seconds before the impacts stopped, and in that time the Machine of Antrikaumora had already lost half its power.

Helesys switched off the Machine. A sandstorm of powdered black glass swept past them. Shawn and Helesys covered their mouths. Comforting power flowed back to her gauntlet—the metal arm and her wand had responded in an instant.

When the smoke cleared, a pockmarked battlefield lay before them. Pieces of meteor that survived radiated steam from the craters—some were little more than fragments, while others were the size of barns. Helesys couldn't help but marvel at the destruction, and hoped that she had seen the limits of the Wolf King's power and not merely the beginning.

Across the field, the Wolf King stood unperturbed. Waiting.

Taunauk stepped forward defiantly. "I am Taunauk Aonar! Clanless. Lover of none. Banished from the living realm and embraced by the dead. Vessel of 10,000 Endroggen warriors, a force never seen by the living. I am fury incarnate and my rage is boundless."

If there was any fear within Taunauk, Helesys could not see it, and she echoed his challenge. "I am Helesys Renquinn, eldest daughter of Great House Byyra. Commander of the third army. She who died a soldier's death before I set foot in this dungeon—she who was burned away only to be born again. The Conduit. The Living Weapon."

Beside her, Shawn cleared his throat. "I am Soldei Milent. The Unbounded. A wisp from the Plane of dreams and a nightmare to those in *all* realms who cross us. And you, you piece of *stercus*, have crossed us."

Wordlessly, the Wolf King raised his right hand, and even Taunauk raised his weapons.

The king snapped his fingers, and the sound echoed like a tree felled.

More cracks came, this time from all around the field. The meteors were breaking. All around them, a brood of jagged limbs burst forth from the fragments. Helesys, Taunauk, and Shawn turned back to back as the battlefield became an unholy hatchery.

Monsters rose—many limbed gargoyles of glass. Half-man, half-spider. Masses of limbs and faces. They clambered up the craters, flooding the battlefield.

"What now?" Shawn asked.

Helesys pulled the jade lemur statue from her pocket. "Now we fly."

"No," Taunauk replied, skin glowing with golden light. "You two fly. I will make my own way. Now, go!"

Taunauk roared and banged his axe against his shield. Golden warriors blazed into existence, joining his call. A chorus rang out and, for a moment, the battlefield was filled with blinding light. And as it dimmed, ten thousand glowing warriors stood in the spaces between the monsters.

The battlefield became a sea of brilliant orange and writhing black, and then it boiled as waves of Endroggen spirits and monsters crashed into one another.

Helesys gripped the statue tight and called on the jade lemur. *"Messoris umbra, matris' vellus, ventus equitem!"*

The totem slipped from her hand and grew to dwarf her. The jade lemur stretched its powerful wings, its green eyes narrowed. Helesys hopped on the lemur's back, and Shawn on behind her.

"I didn't want to live forever," he muttered, voice trailing off as the lemur took off.

The lemur flapped and its powerful wings hurtled them into the air. Helesys willed it to climb high above the fray—some of the twisted monsters below stood nearly twenty feet tall and reached for them as they flew. But most were locked in battle with a golden army.

Helesys and Shawn soared over the battlefield and toward the Wolf King. Helesys kindled power and took aim with her gauntlet. She wouldn't be able to use a powerful blast for fear the recoil would knock them out of the sky, but she wasn't about to be an easy target in the sky.

She loosed five blasts—purple power tore across the sky. Four shots careened into the ground around the king, shattering the glass. He raised a hand and swatted the fifth away like a fly.

The king raised his hand, and sickly green energy coalesced around it.

Helesys knew firsthand what it was.

Roll, she commanded, and the jade lemur obeyed. It jerked to the left, rolling over in the sky—

Shawn screamed.

A green lance of deathly energy screamed past them, missing them by an arm's length.

In their first brush with the Wolf King, he'd taken over the wizard Amadeus and used similar beams. They'd been powerful enough to scar Taunauk's ironwood shield.

Even before the lemur had finished righting itself, Helesys fired half a dozen more blasts. The Wolf King was already readying for another shot, but paused to knock away two of her blasts.

Helesys smirked. *So the king wasn't untouchable.*

The king fired another green lance at them, but the lemur dodged it easily. Helesys returned fired. It was a deadly gamble, but they were nearly halfway across the field.

But instead of firing at them again, the king swept his hands for another spell—

And the sky above them boiled. The starless sky grew blotted with rolling clouds. These clouds grew and grew, and it felt like the sky was falling. Fear gripped Helesys, and she forced the lemur downward.

Shawn gripped her waist tight as they dove. "Don't look back!"

Helesys shouldn't have, but she did, and saw dark hands reaching from the clouds—as if the clouds themselves were alive.

The lemur tucked its wings back in a dive, and for a moment they were free falling back to the battlefield, wind whipping through Helesys hair and hood as she held onto the lemur.

They pulled out of the dive at the last moment, soaring just over the heads of the warriors and weaving between the larger monsters. The latter reached out with branching limbs and fractal maws, pawing in vain for the heroes.

Across the battlefield, the Wolf King smiled and raised his hand. Green light came to him.

They were trapped between horrors above and war below.

"Hang on tight!" she yelled back to Shawn.

Helesys kindled a dangerous amount of power and waited. When the king fired the next lance of green, she held on as tight as she could to the lemur and fired to her right.

The recoil shoved her to the left, and she pulled the lemur and Shawn with her. Green death shot past them, barely missing. The lemur flapped hard, struggling to regain control and stay above the battles below.

The lemur squealed as a hundred mangled hands clawed at it. It fought for every desperate foot of air.

Even as they climbed out of reach of the monsters below, the king took aim at them while the grasping clouds descended ever closer.

Helesys fired a barrage at him, and the king stepped to the side, batting away other blasts. All the while, the green power in his hand festered like a wound.

They had nowhere to go.

Nowhere but down.

"Jump, Shawn!" Helesys shouted.

Even as she leapt from the lemur, she fired another barrage toward the king. She hoped it would be enough to distract him or throw off his aim, or to buy her precious moments.

Helesys turned to see Shawn leaping through the air to the other side. She uttered the magic words again as she fell. Felt the flicker of power fade from the lemur—

The green lance blazed in her vision, piercing through the lemur's chest. It didn't have time to struggle or suffer. It merely crumpled and fell like an autumn leaf.

~

Helesys and Shawn fell to the ground. She kindled power both to brace herself and to stave off the numbness she felt from the jade lemur's death. She'd watched it shrink into a mangled statuette before landing somewhere in the battlefield of golden warriors and dark spirits.

Helesys turned as she fell, firing a spreadblast to cleanse a landing area below her. She didn't feel the recoil in her shoulder, nor the pulverized remains of a monster beneath her feet as she landed.

She just hoped Shawn made it down, and that Taunauk was still fighting his way through. They'd made it so far, so many realms unscathed…

"Let's go!" Shawn shouted. Helesys could just make out a silver blur through the battle. He was running toward the Wolf King.

And she wasn't going to let him fight the king alone.

Helesys fought and weaved her way through the crowded field. Spreadblasts cleaved swathes through enemies, while she battered and broke enemies with the Gar of Shéslang. She spun back to back with golden warriors while her strikes fell in rhythm with others. She crossed the field in a deadly waltz.

"Helesys, look out!"

Helesys leapt to the side just in time to see a green lance carve through the battlefield—monsters of glass and golden warriors flaring into green and bursting.

She rolled and blasted away two more spider-like monsters before kindling speed and sprinting through the fray. Her cloak tore free and she slipped the grip of another monster.

Just beyond, she heard thunderclaps, clangs of steel, and a single frustrated growl of the Wolf King.

She couldn't let Shawn fight him alone.

Helesys crossed the distance in a breath, barreling through smaller monsters and knocking ones twice her size.

When she stepped off the battlefield, a large platform of black rock stood before her, some hundred feet square. Half-destroyed pillars marked the corners. In the center, Shawn fought the Wolf King.

Shawn had unleashed his powers. Black wraps hung loose around his arms and silver mist trailed behind him—otherwise, he was a blur. A flurry of blade and dream, and screams.

The king loomed over him, nearly twice Shawn's height and contrasted sharply with the rogue. He was the epitome of control; his hands were empty and moved only slightly—each time Shawn attacked, a white staff of light would flare into existence between the Wolf King's hands and block the rogue's attack, like flashes of lightning in a storm, before fading again. The thunderclaps had not been the sound of magic blade upon magic staff—each time the staff of light appeared, it brought the sound of a storm.

Helesys churned power and compounded it with her spear. She ran toward the fray.

The Wolf King met her eyes, even as he blocked a strike from Shawn that was too fast for her to see.

"Memoriae alterius vitae te sepelient!" he shouted, anger bleeding into his voice.

Walls of black glass rose violently out of the stone. With a crack and a shudder, Helesys's view of Shawn and the king was blocked by a wall forty feet high and nearly as wide. In a breath, the wall was falling toward her, and her eyes widened. Helesys churned power and fired a spreadblast that tore a hole through the wall big enough for her to duck through. Tons of black glass crashed behind her.

Helesys raised her gauntlet and fired a normal shot, but the Wolf King turned to avoid it.

Two more walls rose around the king—not just walls. An entire room. Helesys dodged to the right to avoid one section falling on top of her while she blasted her way through the next.

She stepped through and found a dozen walls rising up around her, as if the King were conjuring a maze to keep them separated. A table and ghostly chairs rose up, and Helesys realized that it wasn't just a maze. The Wolf King was conjuring sections of the castle itself.

Broken chairs flew at her. Helesys batted them away with the spear, then ducked as the massive dining table flew overhead and shattered against the wall back wall.

Through it all, Helesys could hear thunderclaps and see flashes of the Wolf King's staff growing distant. Even more walls rose up between them. These rose higher still, as if the king was stacking rooms atop each other.

Helesys wouldn't be able to fight her way through quick enough to catch them. So she called on her Ring of Winter and pried another spell from deep within it.

"Pontem glaciei!"

A maelstrom swirled around her, and ice grew beneath her feet. Helesys willed herself upward, and the ring obeyed. Then compounded the spell with the spear—instead of merely rising, the pillar of ice launched her into the air and over the walls of glass.

At the height of her leap, she saw Shawn and the Wolf King. They were climbing up a set of black stairs. The Wolf King was walking backward up the stairs as fast as the obsidian steps appeared. Shawn attacked him mercilessly—now he was more shadow than Terran.

Helesys kindled power, turned her arm backward and fired, using the recoil to propel herself toward them. She landed at the bottom of the stairs and ran after them. Stairs crumbled behind her.

Across the castle walls that rose and fell like waves, the Endroggen spirits still warred with monsters. From the growing height of the stairs, Helesys could see the entirety of the realm and the darkness that surrounded them.

Taunauk's ancestors were winning.

She didn't doubt that Taunauk fought valiantly—she just hoped he could reach her and Shawn in time to help them.

Railings of black glass appeared at the edge of the stairs. Chunks of them broke off and flew at Helesys. She batted them away with the Gar of Shéslang.

Helesys grit her teeth. She was tired of chasing the king.

"Murum glaciei tempestatemque," Helesys said. As more stairs rose behind the king, so too did a thick wall of ice.

The king kept backing up the stairs without so much as pausing. Moments later, the ice wall shattered. Shards hung in the air, then melted, reforming themselves into icicles.

With a growl and a wave of his hand, the Wolf King sent the icicles shooting toward them. Shawn ducked low and avoided the barrage of ice. And for that, Helesys was grateful.

Helesys brought her hand to her face and said, *"Immotalem Immortalis."* Fire bloomed from her hand, spreading out and disintegrating the hail of icicles. Not even steam passed through.

But when the fire faded, Helesys's jaw dropped. Towers were rising up along the stairs, climbing into the sky. The sound of glass crunching echoed across the realm as one of the towers cracked in half—

And fell toward Helesys.

There was nowhere to run. The stairs behind her were collapsing as quick as they were made, and Shawn and the king's battle was too ferocious to pass. Helesys compounded her power and aimed at the falling tower. Her gauntlet grew hot and metal rattled in her shoulder. She released and felt the stairs beneath her feet crack with the recoil.

Purple energy pierced the tower, and a swathe of tower a hundred feet long blew out like a dam burst. The tower was split in two, the sections falling to either side of the stairs, but chunks of glass fell like hail—some so big they cracked and broke the stairs around Helesys.

Out of options, she kindled strength and ran toward Shawn and the Wolf King, narrowly avoiding the destruction behind her.

Shawn and the king's stalemate continued in a flurry of blows—a thunderstorm brought to life.. Shawn was a blur as he struck desperately at the king, but for all his fury, the king was unfazed as he conjured the bright staff over and over to block the wisp's attacks.

Helesys drew on every bit of strength she had, pouring it into her body. Compounding it with the magic spear. Time seemed to slow.

As she met the king with the first strike, she realized two things: Shawn was losing himself. His face was barely visible through his haze of power. And the king was in complete control. His every step was measured, every move of his hands smooth and controlled.

They needed to end this quickly.

The king blocked her first strike—the staff of light appeared with a thundercrack. Spear and staff collided with a clang that was nearly as loud. Tremors rattled Helesys's arms, and she felt the stairs crack beneath her feet.

Even with all the strength she could muster, pain seized her joints.

The Wolf King blocked every strike, even as Helesys and Shawn attacked one after the other and the staff of light drowned out all other sounds.

Helesys screamed in frustration. She shunted power to her gauntlet, stepped up to the king, and fired a spreadblast so strong it nearly blew her off the stairs.

The Wolf King slammed the butt of the staff into the stairs. The world flashed white.

~

The next thing Helesys knew was falling.

The black stairs crumbled. Whole sections of the castle were falling apart. The world was a hail of black glass.

A cloud of silver smoke trailed after her, and within, the faintest outline of her friend. Then the smoke faded. Shawn was gone.

As she fell, lights appeared below—the battle between Endroggen spirits and monsters. She had climbed so high that they'd disappeared from view.

Helesys let out a heavy sigh and fought to keep her eyes open. Somewhere beneath her was the stage. Somewhere beneath her was the Wolf King.

Finally, the stone floor appeared—rushing up at her.

With compounded strength, Helesys caught herself easily and rose to find the Wolf King standing before her. Looming over her like a giant. Behind him, the castle grew until it reached up miles into the sky.

"Little weaver," he said. "Little made-thing. What challenge can you possibly offer me?"

Helesys stared down the king. She had never fought a god without her comrades… Shawn was gone, and there was no telling when Taunauk would arrive, so she could not count on stalling. The king was too fast and too strong to fight physically, and she couldn't match his magic or force of will.

She would have to catch off guard or trick him—that was her only recourse.

"*Lente et gravis,*" Helesys said.

But the king already replied, "*Labuntur vincula maledicti*", his mask unmoving. Her spell died in the air.

"Hieme Murum," Helesys said. A shield of frost surrounded her, traced by the ring's icy tendril.

Helesys lunged for the king with bolstered strength and flailing tendril of her ring. The King stood his ground, parrying her first strikes with his staff—

But as her icy tendril struck, she commanded the Curse of Cold FIre. Blue flames washed over the king.

The Wolf King recoiled and screamed—in that moment sounding much more like a Terran than any god.

Then his voice rose, "*I CALL UPON THE QUEEN—*"

Helesys activated the Machine of Antrikaumora.

"*—TO SAVE ME!*" the king shouted, but his spell was powerless, and the curse of cold fire raged.

Helesys felt her own power ebb, her gauntlet grow heavy. Her shield was fading. She turned all her arcane power to strength, but even with it she felt numb within the antimagic field.

But her relief was short-lived. The Wolf King roared and white light began to glow from within his robe, within his skin. It traced his body in spiderweb veins. Helesys felt his own strength growing. The curse of cold fire dimmed—flickered.

The king fell to all fours, howling with rage. His dagger-sharp fingers gouged scars into the floor. His screams became guttural. The back of his cloak pulsed as bones and muscles shifted.

Meanwhile, the Machine of Antrikaumora ticked away, its power fading. Helesys's stomach turned—she had to save its power. She had to hope Taunauk would arrive. Then she could activate the Machine again and he could cut down the king.

Helesys switched the Machine off and the antimagic field dropped. Her icy shield swirled back to life.

The King glared at her, claws flexing against the floor. She had wondered whether he would go back to casting magic once the field dropped… Helesys wasn't sure which form she would rather fight.

Helesys stepped back, taking precious arcane power from her strength, funneling and compounding her whirling shield of frost. The tendril whipped violently in response. It lashed the king across the shoulders and mask, reigniting the cursed flames on his skin.

The king lunged for her, pouncing like an animal and slashing at her. Helesys leapt to the side, and her ice shield caught the brunt of the king's strike. Chunks of ice enveloped his hand.

Undeterred, he bounded after her, his body twisted into the gangly strides of a wolf. Each strike left more ice covering his body and breathed new life to the cold fire curse. But each strike weakened her shield—even with her power compounded by the Gar of Shéslang, she wouldn't last two more strikes.

She had precious little time and options left: If no one returned, then she had to kill the king.

Helesys siphoned as much power as she dared to her gauntlet. Instead of a spreadblast, she condensed her power even further. A spreadblast was deadly at close range, but much of its power was wasted at the edges. Inside her gauntlet, mechanisms shifted, and power focused into a beam.

The king lunged, and his next strike shattered her icy veil, sending her tumbling across the stone floor. Helesys caught herself and rose to her knees in time to see the king sprinting towards her, claws tearing up chunks of stone in his path.

Helesys funneled all her strength to her gauntlet, then compounded it with the spear that pierced a god. Her gauntlet rattled so violently it felt like her teeth would fall out.

All her power into a single beam. Its range would be even shorter than a spreadblast, likely only two feet long and a hand wide. The recoil would probably tear her arm off. It was better suited to punching through ancient stone.

Or a god's armor.

The Wolf King lunged. Helesys screamed.

Before she could shoot, a barbarian roared. The world flashed golden, as if the realm had been cut in two.

An arc of golden light streaked across the realm, thicker than Helesys and stretching up one hundred feet high. It crashed into the Wolf King and sent him hurtling to the side. He roared as he tumbled across the stone platform and into darkness.

~

Helesys's chest heaved and she let the power bottled in her gauntlet fade enough to control it. Sweat dripped from her forehead.

She glanced over her shoulder and found Taunauk standing beside her. He held his massive battleaxe with two hands, leaving Everfall on his back. His skin and his eyes blazed with golden light, as if he was about to burst into flame.

Behind them, the battlefield was nearly empty. The monsters were broken and beaten—most were dissolving into black glass. The last of the Endroggen spirits were running to Taunauk and merging with him. Ten thousand souls of Accaelum brought to bear.

In spite of her exhaustion, Helesys breathed easier. "Glad you could make it."

Taunauk merely nodded. His eyes were fixed on the darkness, as if he were about to burn holes through it.

A laugh echoed from the darkness. Low and menacing. The Wolf King stepped out from hiding. He stood tall again, his animal form abandoned.

"Most impressive, Taunauk," the king said with only a hint of sincerity.

Taunauk growled and leapt at the king. The king stepped to the side, narrowly avoiding Taunauk's axe. An arc of power swept past him and cut chunks into the castle behind them.

The king stepped forward, blocking Taunauk's next strike with his staff of light. Thunder echoed through the realm, and Taunauk's arc of power was sent astray. Taunauk attacked thrice more in a breath, but each time the king blocked him. Arcs of power flew wild, each colliding with the castle.

The castle crumbled, the tops of it listing overhead until it blotted out the dark sky.

All the while, the Wolf King laughed.

Then he spoke in the dread voice. *"STILLBORN GRASPING HANDS."* The tumbling bricks of the castle writhed as they fell, turning to a million outstretched hands.

"Taunauk, move!" Helesys shouted, but before she could run, obsidian hands reached up from the ground and grabbed her legs. She struggled in vain as even more hands flooded the stone and reached up to her and Taunauk.

A world of darkness was collapsing on Helesys—dragging her under. Threatening to drown her.

And in the darkness, she touched her Rage. Helesys grew mighty, and answered in the dread voice, *"NO."*

The hands around her legs fell free. The hands above and before dissolved into a flurry of black powder.

Helesys had touched that power before. Tapped her rage that was born in darkness—in the agony of her death on the

Eternal Battlefield. Helesys clung desperately to that feeling of darkness.

Helesys reached out to Taunauk. *"Amplificare potentia!"*

Eyes half-closed, Helesys bolstered her friend's power. She felt his strikes, felt his rage, felt the thousands of spirits lending their strength—this was more. He relived memories with each swing of his axe: A lost child, a forgotten name, a cherished moment, each borrowed from his ancestors and each lived as vividly as if he were there. The emotion and Rage of each attack compounded with his ancestors, and each swelled his chest as if he might burst.

She'd bolstered her comrades before, but now, she nearly lost herself in Taunauk's emotions. He was a bottled storm set free. Taunauk's axe became a blur. The golden arcs of power screamed off the blade of his axe and reached up to the distant sky.

The king backpedaled now—stepping wildly. He blocked some strikes and sidestepped others. Then two more strikes sent him sliding back across the stone.

But through it all, Helesys felt Taunauk falter. He was struggling to hold the combined power of the spirits and his rage. His strikes grew reckless, and Helesys feared he might collapse at any moment, though he didn't stop—wouldn't stop.

They wouldn't win. Not like this.

In the darkness, Helesys kept hold of Taunauk and reached out for the seam. She felt not one, but thousands—thousands of worlds. This realm was falling apart, cracking through the center, and so peering through to other realms was easy.

She looked for Shawn.

She looked for wind and dreams. Her mind drifted back through stone halls, flooded ruins, desolate forests, and twisted landscapes.

Helesys wasn't sure how much time had passed, but she found Shawn flying across the frozen tundra beneath the God-peak. He was little more than a cloud of silver smoke, but when Helesys called to him, he turned to her—

She pulled him back to the throne room.

Shawn appeared next to her, a wild smile on his wispy face. "Took you long enough," he said.

Helesys handed him the Machine of Antrikaumora. "Go!"

He took the Machine. It took him only a breath to pull his rapier—Mother's Tears—from his ethereal pouch and plunge into battle.

Meanwhile, Helesys stood at the edge of the stone, embracing the darkness. She continued bolstering Taunauk, but for Shawn, she anchored him to the realm. He was already unbound and at the limits of his power.

The Vessel and the Wisp fought the King, bathing the realm in cataclysm. With each strike, Shawn's sword stole more and more of the King's power.

The king grew desperate and roared in the dread voice, *"FINGERS OF BONE!"*

Fear gripped Helesys's heart. She'd nearly gone deaf from the thunderclaps, but the next sound sounded—felt—as if the realm was tearing itself apart.

White spires rose through the stone. They were sharp as dagger points, but quickly rose as tall as the sky and thickened to the width of castle towers. The sound was somewhere between tearing paper, ripping flesh, and a woman's scream, and so loud that Helesys heard nothing else—not even her own panicked breaths.

Six spires pierced the realm, narrowly missing Taunauk and Shawn.

The king disappeared behind them, trying to use them to split his enemies, but Taunauk and Shawn were relentless. Helesys sprinted around to keep the battle in view.

As Helesys ran, she felt her own strength ebbing. It was taking almost everything she had to help her comrades. They were desperate. The king was desperate. The battle would be over soon—whether they won or whether they died.

The five white towers receded and then pierced the realm again, like dagger fingers stabbing through cloth. But each time, Taunauk and Shawn skirted them and gave the king no respite.

Helesys legs grew shaky, and her vision narrowed. She'd touched her own Rage and it wouldn't be enough.

But she felt something else… Something leaking through the holes pierced in the realm. It felt like the ground up souls from the river of glass—

To Helesys, it felt like untapped strength, and she drew on it.

The Wolf King roared, and yelled in the old words, *"Scindo!"*

Helesys's eyes widened as she felt the seam of the realm tearing open with the king's command. She said in the dread voice, *"NO."*

The seam stilled and finally slammed close.

The king glared at her from across the battlefield. And in that moment, an arc of Taunauk's slash slammed into the king's chest. The king stumbled back, clutching his wound.

Shawn triggered the Machine. The king's staff flickered.

Thrice more, Taunauk struck. The king reeled and fell to his knees.

"Scindo," he gasped, but his words died on his lips. No magic would save him while the Machine was activated.

Shawn plunged a jeweled dagger into the Wolf King's chest and held it there. The white towers slid out of the realm, leaving the stone bare.

Helesys finally relaxed her power and fell to her knees on the stone. They'd done it. She kept her eye on the king in case he tried to flee one last time…

But he only gasped and coughed. The sound was wet and horrid, as if he were already choking on blood.

The Wolf King slumped to the ground.

And started to laugh.

~ ~ ~

What Happens Now

The world went dark around the heroes. Even the stone beneath their feet disappeared.

Helesys felt the subtlest feeling of flying, like something pulling her gently upward. Across the darkness, Taunauk and Shawn reacted with similar disbelief.

So did the Wolf King. He laughed and looked at his hands as he too was pulled upward. His mask fell away and tumbled into darkness, revealing a smooth, bone-white face and pale eyes.

Helesys's stomach wrenched, and immediately after she rekindled her power—

But it was too late.

She could no longer see the Wolf King or her comrades. Then she could no longer feel them.

She was utterly alone, surrounded by darkness.

Before she had time to contemplate the sensation, a new world came into view.

~

Helesys was standing on a mountainside. A grassy slope stretched out before her, descending to the crook of a valley and a forest beyond. The wind was biting, but not unpleasant. Sun warmed her...

The sun.

Helesys stared up at the sun, mouth hanging open. Awe overwhelmed her.

In all the realms, the sun had never risen. Even on the endless sea, the sun had been absent from the blue sky.

They were no longer trapped in the dungeon. They were free.

Tears welled up in her eyes and she blinked them away. A weight lifted off of her and Helesys breathed deep. Savored *real* air.

In truth, this was only the beginning of her struggle. Helesys still needed to journey back to Novissimé and confront her sister Aradi. But standing on the mountainside... Helesys was too tired. She didn't even know *where* she was. Novissimé might've been on the other side of the world—No. This was respite enough, for now.

She couldn't have done it without her friends.

Helesys turned and found Taunauk beside her. He was staring across the valley. Though he stood stoically, he too was on the verge of tears. Helesys knew why: This was the start of her journey, but it was the end of his.

Taunauk glowed softly, and golden motes of light whisked from his shoulders and floated up to the heavens. They came faster and faster, glowing even brighter as they climbed into the sky. Ten thousand Endroggen poured out of Taunauk, and for a moment, it was like stars outshone the sun.

Soon, the sky dimmed to normal, and the outpouring of souls became a trickle. Helesys looked to Taunauk. He stood with his eyes closed as the final souls left him. Sweat beaded on his face and he breathed heavily.

Finally, one last soul emerged, and a glowing vision of Rehkoros stood beside his son. Taunauk met his father's eyes, but could only meet them for moments at a time.

"You've done the impossible, balac. You saved our people. Accaelum smiles upon you."

Taunauk nodded and his eyes fell to the ground.

"Speak," Rehkoros said softly.

"This is all I've known. All my life… What do I do now, father? I have no path."

Rehkoros laid a hand on Taunauk's shoulder. "You are no longer the Vessel. No longer Aonar. You forge your own path, your own name. Live the life that was denied to you for so long. One day, we will welcome you into Accaelum."

Rehkoros's words seemed a cold comfort to Taunauk. He stood still, fists clenched at his sides. His lips quivered, and he could scarcely contain his turmoil.

"Son…" Rehkoros waited for Taunauk to meet his eyes before he continued. "All fathers one day leave their sons, but it has been my greatest honor to see you grow and to fight beside you. I shall miss you, balac."

"I shall miss you, athair." Taunauk whispered.

Both men bowed their heads, and Helesys had been about to bow hers. She knew the prayer of the warrior's prayer of the Endroggen, but Rehkoros did not say it.

"Trust in yourself," Rehkoros said. Taunauk looked as confused as Helesys did. "I love you, son."

Taunauk's face quivered at Rehkoros's words. He reached up to hug his father, but Rehkoros was already fading away. Taunauk's hands grasped air.

Taunauk fell to his knees, overcome by weariness and emotion. Helesys knelt beside him quietly. She didn't know what to say, but she hoped being there would be enough.

Minutes passed before Taunauk's breath steadied. Only then did he echo his father's words.

~

When Taunauk had recovered, Helesys looked past him.

She expected to see Shawn, but the rogue was nowhere to be found. She scanned the sky and reached out her magic sense, but saw and felt nothing.

She stood and surveyed the mountainside, but there was no sign of Shawn—

A tall figure in a blue robe stood solemnly overlooking the valley. Helesys's stomach turned. She knew who it was.

As if sensing her stare, the Wolf King turned to face them. As he did, Taunauk stood, growled, and slipped weapons from his sling.

The king's mask was gone, his hood pulled back. His face was pale white and hairless, like skin stretched taught over a skull. His eyes were milky. He must've been eight feet tall, for even as he stood lower on the slope, he nearly looked Helesys in the eye.

"Thank you," the Wolf King said softly. "Thank you for setting me free."

Power flared in Helesys at the sight of him, but the sincerity of his words stopped her. "What do you mean?" she asked. Beside her, Taunauk was poised and ready to attack.

The king held up his hands in a show of peace. They were thin and trembled slightly. "I bear you no no ill or malice… Please, sit with me, and I will explain everything."

"Where is Shawn?" Helesys asked, her words barely re-strained.

The king hung his head for a moment before meeting her eyes again. "Your friend is still inside. He's the next king."

~

Finally, Helesys and Taunauk sat on the green slope across from the king and listened to his story.

"In the beginning, there was only the Gatekeeper and her realm. Souls wandered in, and though they were trapped, they did not suffer—not as you have seen. One might've called her merciful. But it was not meant to last.

"As the realms grew, so did her interest in her subjects. She grew to relish in their lives. She fed on them—not just their lives, but their emotions. Eventually, she discovered the most potent of emotions: *Suffering,* and all its many facets.

"She fed on us. Grew powerful beyond measure, but the more she grew, the more twisted her appetite became…" The king trailed off, and Helesys couldn't tell whether he was losing himself in thought or whether his newfound freedom was taxing him.

Helesys said, "How do you fit into all this? Did you try to control *her?*"

The king smiled, thin lips parting to reveal sharp interlocking teeth like a shark's grin. "Oh Helesys Byyra. I never controlled the Ungodly Queen. The best I or any king could do was to temper her appetite."

Taunauk stirred, and Helesys asked, "What do you mean, *any* king?"

"I was not the first," he said. "Nor will I be the last. I was *Chosen* once, just like you. Me and my warband fought our way to the center of the realms. I, too, was told that my hand must slay the king. Lies… I struck the killing blow against a king who wielded cold fire and was imprisoned."

Helesys shook her head. "The Voice at Meridian… It wasn't the Queen begging for help…"

"It was me," the king said. "An unfortunate ruse. One I learned from the king before me, and he from the king preceding him. I guided you as best I could: Led you to the Machine, left the Gallery of Memories so that you would be prepared when you journeyed to the heart of the realms… Would you have challenged me, had you known the truth?"

Helesys searched her memories. She forced herself to breathe slowly, to control herself. These were not all the answers she needed.

She thought back to the Machine of Antrikaumora and the ruins beneath the endless sea. "Who was Sinatin Koh?" she asked.

The king held up a bony finger. "We're getting ahead of ourselves. When the Queen was alone, one Terran won her over. He formed a pact and gave himself to her completely. Sinatin Koh was the first king."

"Why make the Machine then?"

The king laughed solemnly. "As a means to escape. Sinatin Koh was a just ruler, but immortality is a curse. The Pact of Kings allows a Chosen to kill us and take our place, but the powers of the Ungodly Queen make the king mightier than almost any mortal. Sinatin Koh made the Machine so that he could more easily slain. All the kings after him kept it, so that in death they could one day escape from bondage." He sighed. "I am sorry, truly. If truth would've set me free, I would've chosen it."

Helesys shook her head. "So, Shawn's in there? Trapped?"

The king tilted his head quizzically. "Are you so sure he's trapped?"

Taunauk glared and answered, "He was tricked."

"He was seeking to return to Eluthiya," the king said. "He wanted his godhood again. At least in there, he has a semblance."

Helesys narrowed her eyes. Sala Gahenna was a hell compared to Eluthiya. "Tell me truthfully, do you believe your own words?"

A weariness overcame the king. His shoulders slumped, and he looked as if he might fall forward. "No. You are right, weaver. All charges are not created equal. No doubt, Soldei Milent feels cheated. But cast your thoughts aside. There is no changing the past."

Helesys and Taunauk shared an uneasy glance, and she saw her frustration mirrored in his eyes.

"Why Shawn?" she finally asked. "The Voice… *You* told him he needed to strike the killing blow. Was that just a lie too?"

The king leaned back, eyes narrowing. Helesys thought he might be offended by her words, but it was hard to read the thin white skin of his face.

"Not a lie…" the king muttered. "The queen *wanted him*." When he saw the confusion on Helesys's face, he continued. "Do not ask me why. I can no sooner tell you why the winds blow or why some saplings die while others live. The queen and the old gods are not beings that can be understood. A mouse has better chance of understanding why Terrans build castles and poison the rodents that wander in."

A pit formed in Helesys's stomach, and was quickly replaced by rising anger. The queen—that thing—had Shawn. Her friend was trapped.

"We can't leave him there," Helesys said.

The king shook his head. "There is no saving him, child."

Helesys met his eyes. "Seems pretty easy to me. We go back in."

"Who will slay him? Who will take his place?" the king asked earnestly. "What will you do if he doesn't want to leave?"

"We'll beat him," Helesys said, keeping her voice level. She dared not show doubt. "We beat you."

The king laughed low. "I wanted to die… I will tell you both this: Time does not flow the same inside as it does here. For the minutes we've sat, a thousand years might've passed inside. There is no telling whether Shawn will be glad to see you or whether the godling will relinquish his throne. Even if you could defy the queen's rules and all three leave… You will not be Chosen. You will be hard pressed to make it to the heart of the realms again.

"In short, the world is stacked against you, Helesys Byyra."

Helesys stood and looked out over the mountain slope, trying to steady her breathing.

They had come so far, struggled and overcome so much…

Tears welled up in Helesys's eyes as she looked over the slope of the mountain, the valley and forest beyond. She closed her eyes and savored the feeling of the sun on her face.

They had come so far *together*. Even though she and Taunauk had walked those first tentative realms without Shawn, she couldn't imagine leaving him there. It had been hard enough those scant times they had been reborn apart from him; Shawn had echoed her feelings.

She couldn't leave him there. Helesys had felt that way even before speaking with the former king, and now her mind was made up.

Helesys turned to Taunauk and found him standing a few steps away. He too was looking out over the landscape… but she saw doubt hanging heavy on his face.

The former king stood, once again towering over both of them. He gave a shallow bow. "I can see that you need time to speak… I will give you space. I've waited centuries for freedom. I can wait a little longer if I am needed."

~

The former king walked down the slope to give Helesys and Taunauk privacy. He stopped some hundred feet below and sat meditating.

But Helesys's eyes were fixed on her comrade. Taunauk looked out over the horizon with a weary soul. In all their journey, he hadn't looked so defeated or so tired. Even when Taunauk was dying, he'd had a defiance to him. Now he looked as if he'd carried the weight of the world upon his shoulders and had done so throughout the many realms.

In a way, Taunauk had done just that.

Taunauk said, "I can't feel them anymore. It's so… quiet."

Taunauk's entire life had been about rescuing the stolen souls of his ancestors. His childhood had been forfeit, filled with training and isolation. As a young man, he'd abstained from everything but growth. He'd left his tribe behind and walked selflessly into Sala Gahenna without complaint. He'd fought and died to free his people. He was powerful and tireless, and Helesys could not imagine someone she would rather have been trapped with.

But it looked as if he could barely stand.

"I owe you more than can be repaid," Helesys said. "You once called me your shieldsister… I am going back for Shawn; I will not ask you to help me."

Taunauk's gaze fell, and he sighed. For a moment, Helesys thought he was relieved.

"You're my friend," Taunauk said. He turned to her, standing up straighter as he did. "You're all I have left. I will follow you to the end, wherever it may be."

For a moment, Taunauk's old strength shown—some of that impossible power he'd borrowed from his ten thousand ancestors. There was no doubt or question on his face.

Helesys's eyes watered, and she nodded. "Thank you. I can't do this alone."

"Nor could I."

~

Helesys and Taunauk wiped their eyes and looked down the hill at the former king. As if sensing them, the king stood from meditating and walked up to them. The tall Terran stopped some feet down the hill, so that stood eye level with the two heroes.

"In all my time as king, I never knew of anyone who escaped a second time," the king said. "You're fools… but I see that nothing will change your minds."

The king reached thin, pale fingers into his robe and pulled out a necklace. A thin medallion hung from it, depicting three wolf heads. The king pulled the cord over his head and held it out to Helesys. She took it.

"I was the third king. Soldei Milent is the fourth. Time passes differently inside, and many years may have passed for your friend. When you find him, show him that necklace to remind him of the kings that came before." The king looked from Helesys to Taunauk and back. "Goodbye."

"Wait," Helesys said, slipping the necklace into her pocket.

"You should not dawdle. The Queen will not stay here for long. She is a wanderer, and there's no telling in what realm or in what time she will appear next."

"Where will you go?" Helesys asked. Beside her, Taunauk looked just as curious.

Though the old king looked like a shadow of his former self, Helesys imagined he was still a capable mage. She was hesitant to let him go, lest his ambition get the better of him.

A smile passed over the king's sharp teeth. "Fear not for your world, Helesys Byyra. I was god, for a while, and I have ruled enough for one lifetime." He looked off over the valley and added, "I think I'll go home."

With the wave of his hands, the king cast one last spell in the old words. *"Suscipeme in domum suam."*

The king faded away, leaving Helesys and Taunauk standing alone.

~

They stood for a long while on the slope. The sun had already fell behind the mountain, and darkness was covering the valley and forest below. Both heroes quietly contemplated what they were about to do.

It wasn't until shade covered all that they could see, that Helesys formed her plan.

"I have an idea," she told Taunauk. "I don't know if it's going to work."

Taunauk slowly drew his eyes away from the landscape and nodded. Resigned to their fate.

Shortly after the king had left them, Helesys wondered how they would find Sala Gahenna again. It was a short-lived question—

For as soon as she wondered, Helesys felt a darkness beside her. She had shivered, and tried not to look behind her.

Whether it was a brief mercy of the Ungodly Queen or Helesys's own numbness, she hadn't felt the horrid and oppressing thing that lurked behind her. Now, even without looking, Helesys could feel the dungeon looming behind them. It would be taking up most of the mountain peak.

Out of the corner of her eye, she saw the mountain shimmer, saw the veil of the dungeon. Slowly, she turned her head—careful not to look directly at it. It took up the entire mountain peak.

And though she couldn't see past the veil, she knew what lurked there:

A pocket world where realm after realm of death and rebirth awaited them, where lingering death grasped for them. Where the Ungodly Queen had tricked Shawn and trapped him.

But in this world the queen was little more than thinly veiled horror. Behind the veil, her form was titanic and monstrous. A writhing mountain of drowning faces and hollow eyes. A nightmare from which they had barely escaped and resolved to dive back into.

Without moving, Helesys asked Taunauk, "Are you ready?"

He stood beside her. Both of them stared at the same spot on the ground—knowing that as soon as they looked upon the dungeon, they would be trapped again.

"I am with you," Taunauk replied.

Helesys nodded and fought to steady her breathing.

Together, they turned.

Until that moment, Helesys hoped for several things: That the veil would part to reveal darkness, or that it might part and reveal Novissimé again, as it did in the heart of the dungeon.

But when she turned, she saw Sala Gahenna in all its unholy glory. She didn't have the chance to scream.

~ ~ ~

God for a While

The Wavering King walked the halls of his castle. He ran his fingers along the stones and trailed wisps of smoke from them. The stone dissolved beneath his fingers, fading to dreams.

Eventually, everything faded to dreams.

And in time, they would fade too. Everything did.

It was hard to look upon the castle or his subjects any other way.

He continued until he came to a balcony. He stepped out into the billowing wind and stood beneath the endless night. Beneath him, the Wode stretched out nearly to the horizon. To the right, the Endless Sea swirled with storms. Over the many years, he'd watched the shoreline swirl and dance, sand giving way to tide, tide to sand.

And there were so very many changes—only some notable to the tired king:

The spider king, Paraxnae, whom Shawn had so thankfully missed an audience with, had wandered into the realm of the fishmen and taken over the hydra, embedding itself in the serpent's back. Not long after, the abomination had escaped to the depths of the endless sea and battled the kraken that guarded the ruins of Antrikaumora. They fought and retreated, circling each others' territory for decades, neither able to kill one another. Even now, they were eternal enemies.

The Deacon of the Wode, whom he'd heard stories of, continued lording over his small village. Though when each piece of flesh he molded into something new, he took a little more of his subjects—dividing their souls more and more until he was surrounded by husks. In death, his people might've found solace… Still, the Deacon refused to leave.

The former Green Knight—tinged with death—now wandered the astral wasteland at the edges of the Ungodly Queen's domain. Even the king could not see her well or how much was left of her sanity.

The barracks had collapsed, crushing Zhug and the hundred goblins that called it home. They were scattered between the realms. The goblins would find homes—even Stizzai—but Zhug would wander, for he was robbed of all his treasure. Zhug had been a mighty ogre, but his intelligence had come from a magic crown that he'd fashioned into an earring. Without it, he wandered blindly and terrorized many realms until he came upon a benevolent wizard, Amadeus.

Amadeus finished his jade egg, his own private realm to call home. He took pity on his fallen friend, and took Zhug with him. It warmed the king's heart to watch them make a home out of the realm—Zhug hauling stone for dwellings and logs for timber while Amadeus worked to craft his friend a new trinket to bring back his mind. In time, he would succeed.

Pitiful Lull, Amadeus's former assistant, remained scattered across the realms in his many copies. He skulked about some whilst finding quick deaths in others.

One-Mind would create its own realm as well… Can such a thing be called an escape?

The Idnauthi would drift the endless night sky until it gave way to the astral wasteland. They crashed and perished, destined never to return to the Queen's benevolent cycle of death and rebirth.

The god serpent Shéslang found a similar end. It shrank until it was small enough to fit in the king's hand, and then it finally lost its mind to the *Duoausongur*.

The Wavering King had considered quarantining the realm overrun by the parasite and Mr. Mask's former realm overrun by the faceless, but the Queen wouldn't allow either. It was then that he learned that lingering deaths were useful to his goddess—in a morbid sense, they helped with digestion.

The Weeping Rent had retaken the barrows, and the Cuckoo continued to grow… It was unlike the other lingering deaths in that one day it would become something like the dungeon—like the Ungodly Queen. The thought made the king shudder.

He felt thousands upon thousands of souls filtering through the dungeon, being trapped, dying, reborn, and finally dying for the last time. To him, it sounded like rain on a tin roof.

He sighed. It was tiring to extend his perception so far, but his control had grown since he'd taken the throne.

Years… and yet they'd passed in a blink—

"Shawn…"

The king stopped. He hovered in the darkness between worlds, gray mist floating from his body.

"Soldei Milent…"

He felt an echo of his old life. A sorceress and a barbarian returned to the dungeon—to *his world*.

"No," the king said aloud, voice hoarse. He hadn't spoken in years. His heart raced, and he searched the realms for them.

The Wavering King found them. They had come back and were reappearing in *the hallway.*

For the first time since ascending, he was angry.

~ ~

The first thing Helesys knew was falling.

She twisted to land on her feet and tucked into a roll, power already kindled in her metal arm. When nothing came for her, she stood and looked out over the dusty, familiar room.

It had been several deaths since she'd seen that humble room and the long, torch-lit hallway. Helesys found comfort in it—which surprised her.

It had been hard to come so far, to stand on that hill and feel the warm sun of freedom, and to realize she had so much further left to go. Even if she made it out again, she still had to confront her sister. And—Movernus willing—mend the wounds left behind in Novissimé.

Taunauk landed beside her, catching himself through sheer strength alone. He stood tall, a mountain of a man beneath his fur cloak. Only moments before, he'd looked beaten and broken after losing the spirits of his people. Now, he looked how Helesys felt—

Ready for whatever came next.

Helesys had called for Shawn in the darkness and heard nothing but silence. Now, she called out again, "Shawn… If you can hear this, come to us. We have to talk."

"Yes. We do."

Helesys and Taunauk whirled around to find Shawn standing before them.

He looked almost exactly as before they left. His eyes a piercing blue beneath his dark robe. Even his forearms were still wrapped in black bandages—

But Shawn's face was twisted into a sneer.

"How dare you," he said, his voice hoarse. "Why would you come back?"

"We're taking you out of here," Helesys replied.

"I gave everything for you! Did you come back just to throw it in my face?"

"I have a plan."

"That's rich. Does it involve killing me? Because I'd like to see you try." Shawn leaned forward, hands in the pockets of his vest. "I don't even need the blades anymore. I was a god, Helesys Byyra. I was a god *before* I took the throne. Do you know what that makes me now?"

As Shawn's words grew louder, Helesys was tempted to kindle strength, but she relented, and finally let it go completely.

"I'm not here to fight you, Shawn. We came back for you."

"Shit lot that's going to do you. You come back for me and take my place. *Then* I feel guilty and come back for you. Meanwhile, Taunauk's stuck with keeping both of us company. Is that it?"

Taunauk grunted. "Are you done?"

Shawn stared him down. "No. I gave my life for you both, and you *came back?*"

"I have a plan," Helesys said again.

"To do what, exactly?"

"How long have you been here, Shawn?" she asked.

"I... It's been seventy-three years."

"It wasn't even sun down yet in the real world when we came back," Helesys said. "Once you told me that you wanted to be a god again, but not like this. This isn't what you wanted."

Shawn's gaze fell to the floor, and then he turned to the meager room. "You know, for a while I wondered why I didn't just untie my wrappings while I was still in the real world. It was stupid—that's not how it works. Here, I lose myself and wander between realms; I'm still in the bottle. Out there it wouldn't have been a fast track to Eluthiya. I would've just faded away. Drifted off to wherever forgotten things go before they're lost forever."

"Shawn, this isn't your world. You may be a god here, but it's not your place. We all have to escape from here *together*. I have to get back. I have to fix things. I have to get back to my family and stop Aradi from whatever she's planning. I want to bring an end to the Eternal War."

Shawn nodded slowly. "And I want to go home to Eluthiya… And I need to face Nimicus."

Taunauk stepped beside them. "I'm with you both, and after that, I'm going home."

Shawn chuckled. "I'd say you've earned it, big guy." Then he turned to Helesys. "Now, about this plan…"

~

Darkness enveloped Helesys and Taunauk, and then they left the realm. Shawn assured them it was like flying. Helesys disagreed. She felt as if she were hanging in the air, but there was no sensation of movement. No sensation or feeling at all—

Only the faint pinpricks of light zipping past.

Of all the things Helesys had felt over her journey, darkness was the most familiar. Her former death on the Eternal Battlefield felt close—as if it happened yesterday—and then it was gone again.

The journey in darkness was over nearly as soon as it began. To Helesys, they'd only traveled for a breath, but she knew intrinsically that they'd traveled across the dungeon.

Shawn took them to the astral wasteland—that barren desert of emptiness between the realms. It was there, he said, that they were closest to the Ungodly Queen.

Even when they stood on the dunes, Helesys felt bereft of feeling. There was no wind, no air or smell. Even though she was standing on the dunes, he feet felt numb to the sensation.

"We'll have to be quick," Shawn said.

"Give me the dagger," Helesys said.

Reluctantly, Shawn pulled a jeweled dagger from his ethereal pouch. Its blade was a dark silver, and in the hilt nine dark red rubies were inlaid—two of these glowed with a brilliant light while the others were dim.

It was the dagger that Shawn had used to kill the former king. It was simple magic, really: The gems stole lives. To be stabbed meant instant death, even for a god. But the dagger could only perform the miracle so many times.

Helesys had only seen it for a moment, but she'd figured out the trick. She told Shawn that her plan hinged around him still having the dagger.

Shawn held the dagger and chuckled as he stared at it. "What would you have done if I didn't have it anymore, or if I would've used up the last two charges?"

Helesys said nothing.

She calmly took the dagger, kindled strength, and plunged it into Shawn's chest. One of the last lights winked out as the dagger's power triggered.

Shawn's face paled as he stared at the blade in his chest. "You lied…?"

The betrayal on Shawn's face pained her, but Helesys didn't let herself answer. She couldn't explain her true plan, lest the Ungodly Queen overhear.

Helesys turned her back on Shawn while her friend—the king—fell to his knees. Unlike the Wolf King before him, Shawn didn't laugh.

Taunauk was staring at her and trying to keep a straight face. Beneath his facade was a mixture of pain and confusion that threatened to break through.

"You didn't need me?" he asked.

"Not in so many words, but I needed the gesture. It will give me something to hold on to."

"What are you going to do?"

Helesys ignored the question. "Do you trust me?"

After a long moment, Taunauk nodded. Then he vanished too.

This time, Helesys killed the King. Which meant that the fallen king, Shawn, and her ally, Taunauk, would go free. That was how the curse worked. Helesys would stay behind as the new king.

Only she didn't plan on staying that way.

Helesys stood alone on the dune of the astral wasteland. Her heart pounded in her throat, and she kindled power to calm herself. She calmed as power churned within her.

She was alone beneath a starless sky and in a half-imagined realm—

Then the dunes dropped out from beneath her, leaving Helesys floating in the dark.

~

In the darkness, Helesys felt her sense of her body fall away—her armor, the feel of where her metal arm met her skin, even the soft hum of her wand.

Everything fell away. Everything except the Gar of Shéslang—that she held onto like an anchor.

Helesys had no idea how much time passed before a voice called from the darkness. She spoke in the dread voice—a roar of whining glass, tearing flesh, and roaring fire. It came from all around.

"I just want them to be happy," the Ungodly Queen said. "No one was happy when they came to me… Aren't you happy now?"

Through the darkness, Helesys didn't just hear—she felt the Queen's sorrow and anger.

To fall in love with each creature. To dote on them. To shower them not just with death but life after life, until the stars died and their souls were ground to dust.

The Queen would never leave them, and she would never let them leave.

"I give them a chance," the Queen said. "I could eat them and leave them with their memories—their failures and sufferings and loss…

"I am a merciful goddess. I *TAKE* their memories from them."

Helesys looked up into the darkness. Even though the voice came from all around, she was certain there was something lurking just beyond the veil—

The face of something vast and incomprehensible.

She had felt it before—when she had stared past the gorge of glass and into the darkness beyond. Felt it feeding on thousands of broken souls.

Helesys had been terrified then, and she felt it now.

Somehow she found her voice. "How is that merciful?"

"They are reborn in me. You call this a prison, but it is also a womb for these pitiful creatures to be reborn. Free from the shackles of their old lives, free to become someone else, something new, something *MORE*.

"But you squander your gift. The first thing my children do is search for their memories, try to remember who they were. What is the point of rebirth if they become the same damned soul?"

Helesys asked, "Who are you to decide? Who are you to take from them? They could've been perfectly happy!"

"No one that wanders the world and finds me is happy! *NO ONE!* Taunauk was a shell of a human who would only have a chance at peace once he was rid of his ancestors! Soldei MIlent was doomed to rise to a wisp and fall to a Terran over and over, never finding peace. Here he was a god and no longer damned. You were a broken elf, your very soul and mind torn apart. Do you think that you would've become whole again without me?! And you dare come back—to drag your friends back into this Hell that you so despise!"

In the darkness, Helesys her terror ebb like a tide. Felt anger replace it. "Shawn wasn't free. You took his choice. You took everyone's choice! That isn't merciful. You're just a monster justifying your hunger. What about the lingering deaths? Why create this horrible place? Why not a utopia?"

"There is no salvation without suffering. Would you have risen so high if not for the suffering you've waded through?"

Helesys shook her head. "My gifts and my life are why I'm here. No commoner or warrior could warp the world as I have. I am here because of my power, and *I am done talking.*"

~ ~ ~

Bane of Gods

Helesys faced the Ungodly Queen.

She floated alone in darkness, staring up at a starless night sky.

Somewhere behind the veil of black was the face of the Ungodly Queen. Helesys couldn't see her, but she could feel the *thing*. The Queen was beyond titanic. It felt as if her face—or merely her eye—took up the entire sky.

Even though Helesys no longer felt her wand, she felt power churn within her. Nothing else mattered, save the power within her. She took her inner strength, the power of the king, and funneled it through the Gar of Shéslang. Then she tapped her Rage:

Dying on the Eternal Battlefield and being reborn. The fear upon waking. The confusion, and finally the anger.

Here in that purest darkness, Helesys smiled. She might not have even needed the spear for what she wanted—her rage alone might be enough.

As Helesys grew mighty, the visage of the Ungodly Queen shrank. Her eye no longer encompassed the sky. It felt as if Helesys could see the face of her—

Still veiled by darkness.

Helesys called on the Curse of Cold Fire that dwelled within her. For a moment, the blue flames pushed away the darkness, and Helesys felt her connection to her Rage falter. But she only held it a moment.

She lashed out, sending a tendril of bright blue power up into the sky. It climbed up like a spire, reaching up and piercing the darkness like a tiny star.

Blue fire erupted across the sky as the Queen's face caught flame. As the darkness receded, Helesys saw a vaguely Terran smile—of a creature that could only be described by the mask it wore.

As quickly as the fire spread, the Queen blinked—merely blinked—and the curse died. Darkness came again.

But Helesys had counted on it.

She could never fight the Queen. Helesys had faced several gods as she'd journeyed across the realms, and each had overshadowed her. Even with all her power and rage, Helesys was only mortal.

So she took power from the dungeon itself.

Floating in the space between realms, it was easy to reach into the gorge of glass, where souls were ground up and drip-fed to the Queen.

Helesys commanded the river of souls with the dread voice. *"YOUR POWER IS MINE."*

At first, the realms trembled as flow between them changed—like lilies caught in a surge.

Then Helesys trembled.

The pure power of souls swirled around her on a scale that Helesys could barely comprehend. Power arced away from her in waves that shook whole realms, triggering landslides and earthquakes.

Helesys teetered on the edge of darkness and purest power.

The Queen reached for her—her hand so large that only her fingers were visible. They came down from the sky like six white daggers the size of castle towers—their points converging on Helesys.

For a moment, Helesys sensed something in the Queen: Surprise.

Despite the agony and exhaustion filling her, Helesys smiled and grew mighty.

"NO," Helesys said. The spear rattled in her hands.

The six white towers froze in the darkness—stopped by Helesys's command.

Helesys screamed, "I don't think you heard me—*YOUR POWER IS MINE!"*

All the power of all the realms swirled around Helesys. Thousands of souls, thousands of lives, suffering, pain, death, and rebirth—all of it—came to her.

And into her.

She was a whirlpool at the center of the dungeon and no shred of power escaped. Gar of Shéslang shattered in her hands and she drank it too. Purest agony seared through her body. It felt as if her muscles and bones were expanding, swelling with life. Her veins were on fire. Her skin felt as if the Cold Fire Curse had swallowed her.

Helesys remembered the day she died—the pain and the desperation. The emptiness.

This was no different.

She would not be turned, not be broken, nor denied.

Helesys had abandoned her armor, her spear, her gauntlet, and wand. Now she let her body fall away. She became the embodiment of purest Rage. She embraced the emptiness she'd once found in death, found comfort in it, and grew mightier still.

The Ungodly Queen fought now, with all the desperation of a corned animal. She lashed out at this mortal who had stolen her power—who had somehow grown to be her equal. The Queen felt a fear that she hadn't known since her creation, when she'd attacked and eaten her sibling.

But now, Helesys had swelled with power and the Queen's strikes felt like nothing more than slashes of a sword against Helesys's flesh.

Helesys let the Queen strike her, cut her, stab her. The Queen was killing Helesys, and the weaver let her.

Because the closer Helesys came to death, the more her power grew.

~ ~

Soldei MIlent—Shawn—stumbled onto the hillside. A grassy slope stretched out before him. Beyond that lay a valley and a forest. The sky was painted orange and pink with the rising sun.

For the second time in a breath, Shawn felt like he'd been stabbed—or maybe punched.

He was looking at the sun.

Tears welled up in his eyes from joy and also from staring at the sun too long.

The rogue turned and blinked his eyes and found Taunauk standing beside him. He, too, was looking at the sunrise.

Taunauk said, "I wasn't sure if I would see it again."

Shawn kept looking around the hill.

"Where's Helesys?" he asked.

Taunauk bowed his head.

The hill shook—No. Something behind them, something enormous shook.

Without looking, Shawn knew what it was. It was a thousand faces trapped within a mountain of paper thin flesh—drowning beneath it as they were killed and reborn within the monster that was the Ungodly Queen.

Helesys was still in there. Why had she gone back in?

Did she go back in just to take his place?

"Stupid," Shawn muttered

Beside him, the dungeon shook and then it stopped.

Shawn turned but saw nothing. There wasn't even a shimmer or a veil to mark where the dungeon had been. Now it was gone—wandered to some other far corner of the world.

If they were lucky, it had wandered to some other realm entirely.

Shawn clutched his chest. "Damn her." Now he didn't even have the chance to go back in after her... As the thought dawned on him, Shawn wasn't sure if he *would* go back in. He would do anything for Helesys, but there was a part of him—a much larger part than he would admit to anyone or even to himself—that was afraid of the Ungodly Queen.

After all, Shawn knew better than the rest of them what she really was.

Taunauk sat on the ground and watched the sunrise, axe and Everfall sitting beside him on the ground.

Shawn's shoulders slumped as he stood beside Taunauk. He felt many things, but *defeated* was at the top of that list.

"You know the really sad thing?" Shawn asked.

Taunauk grinned. "No, but I have a feeling you're going to tell me."

"No one will know. There's no evidence. Sala Gahenna was a myth, always has been... No tales will be sung of the monsters we fought, the people we saved or the gods we found. Whole races trapped inside... No songs sung about Helesys."

At that, Taunauk nodded, then said quietly, "When have the songs ever told the truth of the world? How could they? They never capture the desperation of battle or the breaking of a heart. They're merely words and the true song lives in the warrior. One is a candle and a song of a bard—the other is a blazing torch and the roar within the soul of those who lived. I… I miss her too."

As Taunauk's voice faltered, it felt as if Shawn's heart truly broke. Shawn slumped down beside his friend, and felt something jab him in the butt cheek.

"Ow," Shawn said, leaning, and reaching for whatever thing on the ground he had sat on.

It was a wand. Silver and deep purple swirled along the length of it, which was a little shorter than a foot. Shawn had never seen the wand before, but he knew it all the same.

It was Helesys's wand—the very same that had been inside her metal arm. He was sure of this.

He turned to show it to Taunauk, but the barbarian was already looking at it with wide-eyed curiosity. He felt it too.

The wand began to glow in Shawn's hands with a soft purple light.

"Don't forget about me," the wand said in a quiet voice—in Helesys's voice. "I'm still here."

Shawn and Taunauk's faces cracked into confused smiles. "How?" Shawn asked.

"Helesys and the wand were one. Helesys died on the Eternal Battlefield, and the wand used its limited mind to rebuild her—together. We are Helesys… *I* am Helesys.

"We are left carrying our pain and our memories because we know not what else to do with them. Until we realize they can be sharpened into a tool or left behind to lighten the load forward.

"I left my body behind, along with those oldest and darkest feelings of death and rebirth. Those horrible fragments of myself, of trauma, anger, and pain—all that was left of me when I died the first time.

"I have left my demons behind to do battle with a devil."

As Helesys spoke, and the magnitude of her words dawned on him, Shawn thought he felt the sky tremble—somewhere far away. He wiped his eyes.

Taunauk grunted a laugh. "Someone once said that self-sacrifice was the valor of a short-lived race."

The wand—Helesys—echoed their laughter. "Taunauk, I have something to ask of you."

"Name it."

"I need you to carry me, if only for a while."

"Of course."

Shawn set the wand between them, and the three heroes sat on the hill beneath the rising sun. Shawn relished the sun's warmth on his face—more comforting than any torch in the dead of night.

~ ~ ~

Epilogue

In the dungeon, in the darkness between the realms, Helesys was born for the third time as a goddess.

She held the Ungodly Queen in the palm of her hand. With so much power drained, the fallen god was little more than a mass of twisting shadow.

Helesys had once seen how to supplant a king. She had watched Shawn kill the Wolf King and take his place. Now she would do the same.

Helesys crushed the remains of the Ungodly Queen and absorbed it.

Then Helesys set to work.

Of the many things Helesys could do, she could not destroy herself or free those already trapped within her…

She stretched out her senses and influence across the dungeon, felt the thousands of realms. She felt a pang of sadness for the many that were destroyed, for those she could do nothing about. For the damaged realms, she stitched them together so that they would heal on their own.

She visualized herself at the center with worlds orbiting around her like many little stars.

Then Helesys took stock of the inhabitants.

The old gods she kept close to her, circulating around the inner rings of her universe. She could've killed them, but she kept them instead to feed off of. They would sustain her power for eons.

The realms overrun with lingering deaths, she cast out into the abyss, for she had no use for them. In time, they would fade away into nothingness.

Any realm that could be made a home for mortals, she placed on the outer rings of her universe—close enough to affect, but far enough not to tempt her—for she did not want to become the old queen she'd usurped.

And when any mortals perished, through long life or by accident, they were reborn in another hospitable realm with no knowledge of their past. They would live hundreds of lives never knowing of their new Queen. Hundreds of merciful lives.

In the real world, the old queen's mountainous body had once been made of thinly veiled flesh and drowning faces beneath. Now, the faces no longer struggled. They drifted beneath the surface of the veil.

And when the whole of her knew peace, Helesys left the hillside where Taunauk and Shawn were. She disappeared into the stars and drifted through space where no mortal could search for Sala Gahenna again. In time, those stories would fade further into myth.

And when she was done, Helesys felt weary. She had fought so hard, lived so fully, that all she wanted was to sleep. Sleep until she was needed again.

The unfettered Silent Queen slept.

~ ~

Taunauk and Shawn had journeyed far, but now they stood before the enormous doors of the Elven city of Novissimé. Though Taunauk carried Helesys's wand in his cloak, a projection of their friend walked beside them.

It was one of the first new tricks she learned.

Sometimes Taunauk forgot that she wasn't actually walking beside him, as she'd done for so many realms before.

Maybe it didn't matter, so long as she was there. So long as the Endroggen felt warm sun upon his face.

He was alive. They were alive.

Finally free.

Beside him, Helesys's projection and Shawn were laughing.

She asked, "Shawn, are you sure you have time to do this before you ascend?"

Shawn feigned hurt. "Yes, I assure you. Last time I was a mortal, I had a soul-sucking factory job. I'll manage."

It didn't seem real to Taunauk. It didn't feel like their journey was at an end. Not even when the ancient metal groaned and clangs from the immense buried gears shook the ground. Not even when the doors of Novissimé parted and a company of soldiers swarmed out.

Not when Helesys's mother, Wynbella, stood before them as Shawn explained what happened to them and to Helesys. Nor as Wynbella held close the wand that contained her eldest daughter.

Finally, when silence filled the gaps between them, Taunauk spoke up, "I must go." Though there were a hundred elves around them, he spoke only to a weaver and a wisp.

Shawn and Helesys looked to him.

"I must go home," Taunauk said, and they were some of the hardest words he'd ever spoken, for that meant the end of one journey and the beginning of another—

No.

His entire life had been for the purpose of braving Sala Gahenna and rescuing his ancestors. Now his task was complete.

This was the end of one life, and the beginning of another.

Taunauk embraced Shawn and together they held Helesys's wand. Though they couldn't embrace her too, she stood beside them, bowing her head.

Then Taunauk gave her wand to Shawn.

He left without celebration or fanfare. With only quiet tears.

Taunauk began the long journey home. Across the continent, across the sea, and back to the Endroggen plains he once called home and would call home again.

Where Thuldreth and his family embraced him as brother and uncle. Where the tribe embraced him as a hero.

Where Taunauk would start a life and a family truly his own. One unburdened by the weight of the past.

Where one day Taunauk would join his father in Accaelum, and one day Taunauk's children would join him, as well.

~ ~

Undoing the treachery of Aradi would be no easy task, but Helesys had never shied away from something difficult.

The weaver would accomplish a great many things after returning home to Novissimé: Quelled her sister's insurrection, and made herself a new body. All flesh. She had no need for metal anymore. Then she closed the torn seam within the Eternal Battlefield—ending the Eternal War.

At sundown, Helesys and Shawn walked the mountains to the highest peak. At midnight, they stood on the peak of Glarrin, beneath the stars to fulfill one final task.

"Are you ready?" Helesys asked.

Shawn's voice was quiet. "As ready as I'll ever be."

Shawn carried Helesys's old wand—the relic hummed with power. Shawn loosened the wrappings on his arm. His form grew ghostly and faint under the moonlight.

Then, with the power of a god, he called out a challenge to Nimicus—the bane of dreams and enemy of all wisps.

Stars flickered in the night sky as if some ancient evil had heard their challenge.

Shawn eyed Helesys. "Do you really think she'll help us?"

Helesys traced sigils in the air as she began a communication spell—one that would reach out to a part of her she'd left behind. The sigils began to pulse with white light. Helesys smirked.

"She wouldn't miss the chance to eat another god."

The END of
A BATTLEAXE AND
A METAL ARM

Thank you for Reading

I hope you enjoyed reading this series as much as I enjoyed writing it.

If you did, I would massively appreciate a short review on Amazon or your favorite book website. Reviews are crucial for any author, and a starred review or even just a line or two can make a huge difference.

Looking for more Engrossing Fantasy?

Check out more stories set in *Eluthiya*—the dark fantasy universe consisting of *A Battleaxe and a Metal Arm*, the ongoing short story collection, *Tales from Another World*, and the monster hunter series, *The Sword of the Gray Queen*.

On Writing *A Battleaxe and a Metal Arm*

I started writing *Battleaxe* in December of 2020.

It's hard to believe it's already been 20 episodes. Almost two years…

Battleaxe started as a dungeon crawl through impossible realms. An excuse to come up with the craziest places and monsters I could think of. The only rule was that Helesys, Taunauk, and Shawn had to go to a new place every episode, and that I had to figure the characters out as I went.

But, man, it became so much more.

If you're reading this, then thank you. Thank you for coming on this journey with me.

I'm still having trouble believing that we're at the end. Some of these plot points have been bouncing around upstairs since the series began. Man, I had to wait half a year before I even revealed the Wolf King, and then almost two years before he pulled out the meteor strike!

I may have had some of the plot figured out, but it wasn't until I was already seven or so episodes in, right around the Ill-Fated Voyage, that I started to realize some of the themes of the series. I knew some pretty early on, like giving up and remaining stuck. But others, like pushing past trauma, or how much of our past and our family's past do we carry with us, or indecision about what to do with our life… those I didn't realize until Helesys, Taunauk, and Shawn drowned in the Endless Sea.

Call it what you will, "writing by the seat of your pants", or "writing into the dark". *A Battleaxe and a Metal Arm* was a test of that style of writing.

I definitely learned some things about myself over the course of the past two years as this series unfolded. If you've read this far, maybe you learned something about yourself too. Hopefully, like the heroes, you found a little catharsis.

And now, just like them, we need to find a way to live after our quest is done.

Or, you know, you could check out the rest of the Eluthiya universe if you haven't already.

Connect with the Author

If you want to stay up to date on the latest about Samuel's publishing news and blog, check out his website and consider signing up for his monthly newsletter.

www.SamuelFlemingBooks.com

Samuel can also be found on Reddit, Tiktok, and Facebook.

Samuel Fleming is a Science Fiction and Fantasy author.

He grew up in Maryland, spending most of his time swimming and writing. Swimming gave him a lot of time to daydream, so the two hobbies complemented each other well. Idle day dreams turned into stories, some of which stuck with him for years. These days he swims a little less and writes a lot more.

He loves a good story no matter the medium: Books, TV, video games, comics, tabletop RPG's, or podcasts–most of which he attempts to share with his wife and three kids, and occasionally on his blog.

www.ingramcontent.com/pod-product-compliance
Lightning Source LLC
Chambersburg PA
CBHW030649190726
48286CB00008B/2728